EVIL
BEHIND
THAT
DOOR

EVIL
BEHIND
THAT
DOOR

BARBARA FRADKIN

RAVEN BOOKS
an imprint of
ORCA BOOK PUBLISHERS

Library and Archives Canada Cataloguing in Publication

Fradkin, Barbara Fraser, 1947-
Evil behind that door / Barbara Fradkin.
(Rapid reads)

Issued also in electronic formats.
ISBN 978-1-4598-0100-4

I. Title. II. Series: Rapid reads
PS8561.R233E95 2012   C813'.6   C2012-902222-5

First published in the United States, 2012
Library of Congress Control Number: 2012938154

Summary: Handyman Cedric O'Toole sets out to uncover the chilling
secret locked behind the boarded-up cellar door at the farmhouse of
his old school nemesis. (RL 3.2)

MIX
Paper from
responsible sources
FSC® C103567

*Orca Book Publishers is dedicated to preserving the environment and has
printed this book on paper certified by the Forest Stewardship Council®.*

Orca Book Publishers gratefully acknowledges the support for
its publishing programs provided by the following agencies:
the Government of Canada through the Canada Book Fund and the
Canada Council for the Arts, and the Province of British Columbia
through the BC Arts Council and the Book Publishing Tax Credit.

Design by Teresa Bubela
Cover photography by Masterfile

ORCA BOOK PUBLISHERS
PO Box 5626, Stn. B
Victoria, BC Canada
V8R 6S4

ORCA BOOK PUBLISHERS
PO Box 468
Custer, WA USA
98240-0468

www.orcabook.com
Printed and bound in Canada.

15 14 13 12 • 4 3 2 1

Marquis Book Printing Inc.

To my parents

CHAPTER ONE

"Don't touch that!" Barry Mitchell hissed. His breath was hot on my neck.

I jerked my hand back from the door and turned to him. He looked like a ghost, all bug-eyed and white. But maybe that was the light. There were no windows in the basement and the light from the bare bulb hanging at the foot of the stairs didn't reach the corner. You watch enough horror movies, it doesn't take much imagination.

"What's in there?" I asked.

He shook his head wildly. "I don't know."

"What do you mean, you don't know? You grew up here!"

Barry Mitchell and I were a long way from being friends. But I'd known him for thirty years, ever since he laughed at my name on the first day of kindergarten. My mother hadn't done me any favors with Cedric Elvis O'Toole.

I'd never seen Barry afraid before though. Usually he didn't have the sense to be afraid.

Still, I suppose he had a right to be freaked. He'd just spent two years inside Kingston Pen for assault. He'd been home just a few weeks when all of a sudden his parents disappeared in the middle of a snowstorm. The police hounded him with questions every day for a month. Then came the estate lawyers, and they're not the most cuddly guys in town either. Even now, two months later, folks are still whispering.

"I never went in there," Barry said. His eyes were fixed on the door.

"Why not?" I ran the beam of my flashlight over the door, an ugly old pine slab that had never seen a coat of paint. It was wedged into the rough stone blocks of the basement wall and welded shut with cobwebs. It looked like it hadn't been touched in a hundred years. The Mitchell farmhouse was even older than mine, probably built in the 1850s. Who knew how long this door had been here and what was on the other side?

A secret tunnel? A time capsule?

I thought of my own basement, dark, spooky and smelling of rotten earth. A magnet for a kid with a big imagination and too much time on his hands. As a kid I would have been through this door in a flash.

But Barry just shook his head. He was already backing up, heading for the stairs. That's when I saw the crowbar in his hands. He looked too, and seemed surprised to find it there. He laid it down on the workbench.

"Forget it, Rick. We done enough for today. Let's go grab a beer." Then he was up the stairs two at a time and out of sight.

I shoved the door, but it didn't budge. I threw my weight against it. Nothing. Now, I'm only five ten and one fifty after two beers and a plate of wings. But most of that is muscle. Besides paying the bills, handyman work keeps you in shape.

This door was going to be a challenge.

Barry was done half his beer by the time I reached the kitchen. I took the one he held out. I'm not a big drinker, especially at one o'clock in the afternoon. But when Barry Mitchell offers, you go along.

He grinned, trying to shrug off his nerves. "I don't know why I gotta fix the leaks down there anyway. The place has been leaking since before any of them real estate lawyers were born. It's not like it's going to float away."

I sipped my beer and decided not to take him on. Growing up, you learned not to take Barry Mitchell on. Not when he was winding up for a fight.

"I can't see wasting money on this dump. When I sell it, they'll probably tear it down anyway. The land is what they want."

I saw my next month's paycheck slipping through my fingers. I lived a simple life out on the scrub farm my mother left me. But a guy can't get by on a goat, a couple of hens, a vegetable patch and a few sheds of junk. For starters, I really wanted my pickup truck back. That wouldn't happen until I could pay the thousand-dollar repair bill. Aunt Penny said the old death trap wasn't worth a thousand, but she didn't appreciate all the sweat I'd put into it. I admit it wasn't pretty to look at, but I figured the rust holes improved the ventilation.

"Yeah, but it wouldn't hurt to make the place safe at least," I said, looking around the kitchen. Rusty wires hung from the ceiling where the light fixture had fallen out, and the gas stove looked older than both of us put together. "It's a wonder your parents didn't burn it down. A gas leak with those wires, the whole place could go up."

He gave me a disgusted look over the top of his bottle.

"They were pigs. Mom never lifted a finger to clean the place. The older she got, the worse she got. Up all night reading her romance novels and popping more pills than a Hollywood starlet. And Dad...well, you know Dad. What the fuck else is there to say?"

I did know Pete Mitchell. Everybody in the county knew Pete Mitchell. If it was past two o'clock in the afternoon, you stayed out of his way. He had the blackest, drunkest rages I ever saw. And in these parts, that's saying a lot. It was one reason why, even though Barry Mitchell gave me grief, I never gave up on him completely.

My mother left me to grow up like a weed in the garden while she watched her soaps and listened to Elvis. But at least she was harmless. I never had to hide out in the barn waiting for her rages to pass. Or dodge flying shovels when I failed some test I didn't even know I was taking.

This time, Pete Mitchell had taken one drink too many. Valentine's Day, two in the morning, he and his wife got kicked out of the Lion's Head. They headed off toward home on their snowmobile in the middle of a blizzard.

Nobody had seen them since.

Barry popped open another beer and looked across the table at me. His face was all twisted, and for a scary moment, I thought he was going to cry.

"I hate this place," he said. "It never felt like home." He tossed his head back and chugged half the bottle, pausing at the end to drag his dirty fist across his mouth.

"I can't pay you yet, O'Toole. I'm sitting on a fortune, that's what the lawyers say, but unless I sell it, I won't have a cent to pay you."

With the usual O'Toole luck, my great-grandfather had gotten a hundred-acre land grant of the most useless piece of cedar swamp in the county. Barry's great-grandfather had gotten a hundred acres on a point of land jutting into Lake Madrid. These days even the crappiest waterfront shack went for a quarter of a million. No wonder the lawyers were drooling.

"I know," I said, "but working together, the expenses won't be too high. Let's at least fix the leaks and the electrical. After that…" I shrugged, trying not to look too desperate.

Barry drained his second beer.

"That's a plan, O'Toole. Hell, I can't sell this dump yet anyway! My folks' bodies are still out there somewhere, so it ain't even legally mine. So let's drink to the handyman team. Mitchell and O'Toole." He laughed. That creepy Barry Mitchell laugh that used to curdle my blood. "Cedric Fucking Elvis the Tool."

CHAPTER TWO

Barry's old truck was nowhere in sight when I finally showed up the next day. I was late because the seat on my dirt bike had fallen off when I hit a pothole on the way. I'd had to hitch into town for new bolts. Boy, did I ever need my truck back.

There was no note, but I was half frozen from the ride and the door was open so I went in. The place was an icebox. No furnace, no heaters, and the woodstove was a fire hazard. Barry probably went into town just to get warm. The Lion's Head serves a piping-hot Irish stew along with its pitchers of beer.

I headed down into the basement to check out the furnace. It was in the darkest corner of the room but even in the lousy light I could see it was beyond hope. It was an ugly old thing held together by forty years of soot and mold. I didn't think it had been serviced this century. Didn't anyone ever come down here? I grabbed a flashlight and shone it around the room. Wires, pipes and beams all covered in dust. Cobwebs everywhere, beetles scuttling, oily puddles on the dirt floor.

And that door.

Ever since I was a kid, I've been a sucker for mysteries. Always wanted to know how something worked or why it did that or what would happen if I pushed this button. I wasn't one to look up answers in a book. I wanted to see for myself. The worst thing my mother or my teachers could say was, "Don't touch that."

That only got my imagination going. I felt like a magician when I pushed a button and made something move, or put something together so it worked again. When there are no other kids around for five miles and your mother is glued to *As the World Turns*, it's nice to feel like Superman.

I went over to the door and aimed the flashlight along the edge. For the first time I noticed it was nailed shut at the very top by a huge rusty spike. I picked up the crowbar Barry had left on the workbench the day before and went to work on the spike. The door was solid as a Douglas fir. It barely splintered as I yanked and pushed and pried and cursed. Finally I worked the spike loose enough to lever it out. It fell to the dirt with a heavy thunk. I kicked and shoved and threw my shoulder at the door, but it still didn't budge. Soon I was sweating and panting like I'd run a marathon.

But every now and then I remember to use my brain. It works a little different from most folks', and it makes people laugh, but it comes up with a good idea now and again. Okay, maybe not that gas-powered scarecrow or the robot feed dispenser, but inventors learn from each mistake. And someday…

Anyway, now I looked at the door and realized it pulled outward instead of pushing inward. With the crowbar's help, I levered it slowly open until I could stick the bar through the crack and give it a good yank. The door squawked open six inches. Cold dead air rushed out. Air that had been in there for probably thirty years. A couple more yanks and I had it open far enough to look in.

Inside it was dark as pitch. Silent as a grave. I shivered. I didn't want to think what was in there, lurking in the corner or coiled on the ground. Sometimes imagination is not a good thing. I shone the flashlight inside. I was surprised to see just a small empty room with a dirt floor, stone block walls and a low, sagging ceiling of rough lumber and beams.

I squeezed my way inside for a closer look. The walls were lined with shelves of mason jars. They were so dusty and black I barely recognized them. Mouse droppings and cobwebs covered everything. On the floor were some wooden bins half full of weird round things. I reached through the cobwebs to pick one up. It was hard and shriveled, like a black walnut shell. An apple? Potato? I sniffed but could smell no decay, no sweet ferment. Nothing but stale, musty air.

I squatted in the middle of the room, disappointed. No secret passage, no time capsule, no magic kingdom. Just a root cellar where Barry's mother stored her harvest crops. Long ago, when she still cared.

I flashed the beam into the corners one last time, hoping to see the outline of a secret door. Maybe I was being silly but something about this room felt spooky. In the bright light, I could see the walls were scratched and chipped, and the earth dug up. Like an animal had been trying to dig its way out.

I shook my head to get rid of that idea. When I jerked the light away, something pale caught its glare. Against the far wall, almost hidden behind the bins, was a bunch of brown sticks. I moved closer, hunching over because the ceiling was too low to stand. My flashlight played over the sticks. There were different sizes and shapes scattered about. In the middle something curved like a backbone. An animal? Small bits of cloth were spread underneath, as if the animal had built a nest. Trying to get warm? Trying to comfort itself? I swallowed. In the silence of the room, my breath sounded loud.

I picked up a piece of thin cloth. Most of it fell apart in my hands but a scrap remained, dark and rotten but still showing a plaid pattern. I felt sorry for the little animal that had tried so hard to escape and, finally, to keep itself warm. I felt like I was disturbing its soul.

I was just about to lay the cloth back down when I saw something else lying behind the bin. It was round and smooth. Heart pounding, I picked it up and held it under the light. I recognized the shape right away. The lower jaw was gone and the eyehole on one side was cracked. But there was no doubt it was a skull.

Something had been trapped in here and had curled up to die.

I looked at the bits of cloth in my hand and then at the skull. It was larger than the skull of a groundhog. Larger even than that of a skunk or raccoon. It was about the size of the skull of a yearling lamb or a dog.

Or a small child.

CHAPTER THREE

I wanted to drop the skull and get out of there as fast as I could, but I forced myself to slow down. Carefully I set the skull and cloth back where they had been. I pushed the door shut and shoved the spike back in. I couldn't do anything about the mess the crowbar had made of the door, but at least it wasn't obvious it had been opened. As long as you didn't look too hard.

I was hoping Barry wouldn't look too hard.

My heart was pounding loud and fast. As emergency transportation, my dirt bike gets the job done, but it has its problems. It only starts at a dead run, and only if it feels like it. I prayed it would cooperate as I raced it down Barry's laneway. I kept one eye out for potholes and the other watching the turnoff ahead. I was afraid Barry would show up and ask questions before I could make my getaway. Lunch at the Lion's Head, even with a long liquid dessert added in, only takes so long.

But the road was empty. Once the engine sputtered to life, I leaped aboard and gunned it. I raced away from the Mitchells' farm as fast as the cranky old machine would go.

I've lived on my farm outside Lake Madrid all my life. But my mother broke all the family rules by getting pregnant and taking the secret of my father's identity to her grave. So I don't have a huge supply of friendly relatives. Normally that suits me just fine. I'm not so good at small talk or remembering birthdays or kissing babies. But when it comes to getting advice, I don't have a lot of choices. Only one, in fact.

I aimed my bike down the highway toward Aunt Penny's grocery store on the edge of town. Even when Mom was alive, Aunt Penny was the one with the answers. You had to put up with a lot of questions and tongue-lashings before she got to the answer, but usually it was worth it. You just had to brace yourself.

I have no idea how old Aunt Penny is. She's actually my mother's aunt, and she's had steel-gray hair and wrinkles as long as I can remember. Aunt Penny was the only one who tried to give my mother advice, till even she realized it was a waste of time.

From the front window of her corner store, she's like a soldier at the gates to town. Nothing gets by her, and if anyone knows the secrets of the Mitchell family, it's Aunt Penny. All the locals stop by her store.

They might only buy a thing or two, but if it's news or gossip they want, the lineup at the cash is the place to get it. I had to wait while Aunt Penny talked to Gerry Ripley about spring flooding and to Nancy Weeks about Bud's latest chemo.

Finally the crowds cleared out and she turned her sights on me.

"Aren't you on a job?" she demanded. How she knew things like that is always a mystery. I guess since real jobs don't come my way all that often, they stick in her mind.

"Yeah. But..." I glanced around the shop. Quiet for once. I knew I'd better talk fast. "I was just wondering. The Mitchells— did they only have one kid?"

She gave me that look. The Aunt Penny what's-the-real-story look. I'm not really good at explaining myself, and that look never helps. I shrugged. "I mean it's a big house. Lot of bedrooms. I just wondered, you know, if there were other kids. Before Barry's time, maybe."

I thought I'd covered up pretty well, but this time Aunt Penny gave me the eyebrow too.

"Why? Has Barry said something?"

I shook my head quickly. Then I had a stroke of genius.

"That's the thing. I thought I saw signs of another kid, but I don't want to upset him by asking. You know Barry."

The frown disappeared. She sighed and leaned across the counter, like she was sharing a secret.

"Poor Pete and Connie have had more tragedy than any family should have a right to, and ending the way they did...it's just so sad." She bowed her head. "Sad, sad. There were supposed to be other children, Ricky. Connie wanted a whole house full. But the good Lord had other ideas."

It wasn't often Aunt Penny brought up the good Lord. She figured if he was running things, he wasn't doing that good a job and she was better off doing it herself. But sometimes people are funny when it comes to life and death.

"What happened?"

"Started years ago, when Connie lost her first child. Girl, stillborn." She stopped and looked at me. Like she was trying to decide how much to say. "Pete loved Connie, don't get me wrong. But it's no secret he was a drinker, even back then. I'm not saying he caused it. Might have been just the stress of all his yelling, but anyway, the birth was rough. Wrecked up Connie's insides so the doctors weren't sure she'd ever have another. Then along came two boys, Barry and his younger brother, I forget his name. Cute little boy, Connie's favorite. Blond like her, where Barry's burly and dark like his dad.

Things were looking up. Connie was never strong, but in those years I remember she came out of herself."

I was holding my breath, like it would stop the awful thought running through my head. There was no younger brother when Barry and I were at school. Aunt Penny looked sad. Ed Higgins from the bank came in. She didn't laugh at any of his jokes and waited for him to go before she sank back on her stool. She rubbed her arms as if they were sore.

"The little boy got leukemia. It came out of the blue. They took him to the hospital in the city and Connie stayed there with him for weeks. Pete had to be here with Barry, but it was hard on everyone. Back then there wasn't much you could do. I was surprised she ever came back. She was like a ghost. All they had left of him was a little copper urn."

"How old was he?"

"I don't remember. Barry and you were in kindergarten, I remember that. She was never the same after that."

Neither was Barry, I thought. Doors punched in, chairs thrown across classrooms. Fight after fight. By the time he got sent away, no kids were allowed to play with him.

CHAPTER FOUR

The bell over the shop door rang and I turned just as two cops came in. Sergeant Hurley, the commander of the local unit, and behind him Constable Swan. My pulse spiked.

Hurley slapped me on the back. For some reason he was always trying to take me under his wing. Give me advice, like he was my father.

"Well, O'Toole, keeping out of trouble?"

Beneath her cap, Constable Swan's blue eyes twinkled at me. My face burned.

Before I could untangle my words, Aunt Penny piped up.

"Ricky's working for Barry Mitchell. Fixing up the old place for sale."

"Oh yeah?" Hurley said. His grin faded, and I saw a frown cross Swan's face.

"You guys still looking at him?" Aunt Penny asked.

Hurley hitched his pants over his gut. He wasn't a big guy, but he managed to look like a bear in his cop gear.

"Aunt Penny, you know I can't comment on an ongoing investigation. But yeah, we're sending the canine unit out there today, and until we know what happened to them..."

Constable Swan was watching me. Her blue eyes were serious now. She wasn't from around here, so she didn't know all the local gossip, but she caught on fast. It would be so easy to blurt out that I'd found some bones. But the thought of

Barry held me back. He'd be freaked out enough already with the police bringing dogs to nose around.

So I ducked my head and made for the door. I felt Swan's hand on my arm as I brushed past. Her voice was a whisper.

"Be careful, eh?"

I walked out of Aunt Penny's in a daze. My skin felt hot where Jessica Swan had touched it. She'd never in a million years be interested in a scrawny, dirt-poor handyman like me, but it was nice to know she worried. My mind spun as I tried to make sense of what I'd learned. Not just from the cops, but also from Aunt Penny about Barry's brother. I couldn't ask Barry about him. There were too many walls in that family, too many walls in his mind. I needed more answers before I could figure out what to think.

The Mitchell family was another that didn't put much stock in God.

Sunday mornings Pete would still be at home sleeping it off, and I'd never seen Connie in town without him. But if she'd brought back an urn, it should be buried someplace.

I knew it wasn't in the cemetery where my mother was buried, because I knew every tombstone in the place. So I headed to the Protestant church in town, the old one down by the creek. It was a peaceful kind of place, if that's important to you.

In April the trees were still bare, but their branches were beginning to turn green. Some little blue flowers were already out and the grass was full of daffodils. At the bottom of the slope, the creek brimmed over its banks.

I searched the tombstones, looking at dates. Close to the church, the stones were over a hundred years old. Farther out near the parking lot, they were polished and new. Faded plastic flowers leaned against

some of them. I hate walking in grave-
yards, imagining the dead bodies under my
feet. When the cops took me to identify
my mother, the car windshield had pretty
much wiped out her face. But there was
enough of her left that I can't forget.

I shivered. I was about to give up when
I stumbled upon a bunch of small plaques
down by the creek. They were spaced only
a few feet apart, just big enough for an urn.
As I pushed aside the wild rosebushes with
my foot, I read the names. Familiar village
names—Bud's father, Ripley's brother.
Then a plain little stone on the ground.

Louie Mitchell, beloved son.
January 4, 1979–April 20, 1982

Three years old, I thought. About the
size of a yearling lamb.

CHAPTER FIVE

I lay awake half the night, imagining the sound of a little boy screaming in the dark.

By morning I'd decided I was never going back to the Mitchell house. I knew Aunt Penny would kill me for quitting a real job, but I didn't need the money that bad. Spring was here. Spring meant cottagers looking for handymen to fix their decks or leaky roofs, or to get rid of the mice that had moved in over the winter.

It also meant the snow had melted off all the stuff in my yard. Aunt Penny called it junk. I called it supplies. I'm an inventor. A broken lawn mower could have a new life as a winch or a scarecrow. Even a three-legged chair was good for something. I knew everyone in the village laughed, but what inventor hasn't had lean times before he made his big discovery?

It was a sunny day. I sat on my front porch with my dog and my coffee and wondered where to begin. I had six and a half cars and trucks sitting in the mud by the back barn and quite a few junked appliances too. That didn't count the fourteen lawn mowers in my back field. The snow hadn't done them any good. I needed another shed. That's what I'd do today.

Chevy snatched her ball as soon as I got up. She's a border collie that thinks life is one long fetch. I tossed the ball as I walked toward the barn. I heard the phone ringing and thought of not answering it. I almost never get phone calls from real people.

But then I thought of the cottagers. A new job would hold off Aunt Penny.

It was Barry Mitchell.

"Jeez, O'Toole, where are you?"

"I went yesterday. You weren't there."

"I know, I know. I got held up. Lawyers. Cops. Never ends. But I'm here now."

"I don't know, Barry. Not sure it's worth fixing up."

"Let's at least put some nails and a few licks of paint on it." His voice took on a whine. "Help me sell it."

"I got a couple of jobs lined up."

The whine edged up a notch. "Rick, I'm sorry. I gotta get out of this town. I'll never get a break here. Yesterday they brought dogs out here, for fuck's sake."

I held my breath, waiting for the rant. But none came.

"Gave me the creeps," was all Barry said. "There's a thousand bucks in it for you if you help me sell this place."

I looked out the window at my dirt bike parked where the truck should be. Before I knew it, I was caving.

In less than an hour I was back at his place. I was glad to see he was sober. Even smiling. I guessed the cops hadn't found anything.

"We're going to work on the kitchen today," he said, heading inside. "My lawyer says that's where you sell the house or not. So first thing, we're going to get rid of that hole in the ceiling."

I looked at the rusty wires sticking out of the hole in the kitchen ceiling. They were almost touching. One small power surge and *pow*!

"You got any caps for those wires?"

"I figured we'd just shove them back in the hole and put a patch over it. I got the patch."

"But—"

"I'm not fixing up Buckingham Palace here, Rick!"

His face was turning red, so I shrugged.

I grabbed a rickety stool. "Fine. We'll cut the power off at the panel and I'll tape them. Can you go down—?"

"I'm not going down there!"

I was up on the stool by this time, so I decided not to argue. His smile had been paper thin.

"You know what?" I said. "I'm in the mood to paint. Let's start on the cabinets." I find painting calms me down. I was hoping it'd do the same for Barry.

We worked away without talking for a while, taping and sanding. It was peaceful, and Barry even began to smile again.

"Aunt Penny was talking about your folks yesterday," I said. "Remembering when we were kids, all our friends…"

"I never had no friends, Rick."

I had no good comeback for that. Barry had scared off just about everybody. So I kept going. "I even remember your little brother. What was his name?"

Barry stopped, paint brush dripping. "Louie."

"Louie, right. Little blond kid. Must have been hard on your folks."

Barry grunted. Went back to his painting.

"You must have missed him too."

"I don't hardly remember him."

"I would have liked to have a little brother like that." I actually had an imaginary brother growing up. Not as good as the real thing, but all I would ever get. "Did you visit him when he was...you know, sick and all?"

His paint brush went all squiggly on the cabinet door. "I don't know. What are you asking about him for?"

"Just passing the time, Barry. No big deal."

"No." He threw down his brush. The green drops on the tile didn't improve the look any. "What the fuck you sticking your nose in for, O'Toole? What you saying?"

"I'm not saying anything. Just that it kind of explains things, you know? About your folks."

"It was thirty fucking years ago! Louie was here, then he died. I got over it."

I shut up. Bent my head and moved to another cabinet farther away. Barry picked up his brush again, gave a few good swipes at the cabinet door. Green paint smeared the fridge. He cursed, wiped it off, got it on his pants and tossed his brush in the pan.

"Fuck it! I've had enough."

I held up my hands. "Okay, maybe we can—"

"Don't be a wuss, Tool. You're always such a wuss. I'm going out! You do whatever the hell you want."

The whole place shook when he slammed the door.

CHAPTER SIX

I let out my breath. I hadn't even realized
I was holding it. Keeping one step ahead
of Barry could make a guy dizzy.

Painting is not something you can leave
midway through, so I finished the first
coat on the cabinets and cleaned up. It was
peaceful without Barry. Afterward I explored
the house. If Barry came back and asked
what I was doing, I'd tell him I was figuring
out our next job.

But I was really looking for clues.

Upstairs, the master bedroom was over
the kitchen. In these old houses, that was the

warmest place. The sheets looked like they hadn't been washed in a year and the place stank of old socks and piss. Pete's underwear and clothes were all over the floor. Connie's drawers hung open. Underneath the jumbled clothes I found a stash of empty Valium bottles. On her dresser, a small velvet jewelry box lay open. Empty.

In the back under the eaves were two more bedrooms. They'd be cold as an arctic cave in winter. One had a mattress and electric heater on the floor, and a few clothes piled on a homemade bookshelf under the window. The room was full of empty beer cans and frozen-dinner boxes. Barry's cave.

The other bedroom was a junk room, so packed you could hardly open the door. Broken chairs and lamps, a cooler, an old tv with a smashed screen. I discovered a baby crib almost buried by boxes and garbage bags. I poked through these. Nothing but magazines, old clothes and broken dishes.

The crib was the only hint that a child had ever lived here. There were no old Fisher-Price toys in the whole house. No trikes or LEGO or rocking horses.

No pictures anywhere. Even my mother stuck my school photos up on the fridge with an Elvis magnet. It was as if Louie and Barry hadn't grown up here.

As if Louie had never existed.

When my mind gets stuck on something, it doesn't let go, so I searched the rest of the house. Lots of broken old stuff that even I wouldn't keep, but not a single trace of the kids. I found Connie's stash of Demerol and Pete's hidden vodka bottles. I found stacks of romance novels, *Soap Opera Digest* and gossip magazines. Old porn movies stuffed behind the couch. I backed away. It felt wrong to peek into dead people's lives.

Outside I took deep breaths of the clean air. The sun was shining, melting the last of the snow from the boats, quads and snowmobiles in the yard. The barn roof had caved in, but the big shed beside it looked newer. Its door hung open a crack. I opened it wide to let the sunlight in. It looked like Pete's workshop. Tools were hung on the walls, and a pine workbench ran across one end. Boxes of supplies and hardware were stored under the bench.

The workbench was cluttered with junk. Tools, bits of wire, loose screws, empty oil cans and greasy work gloves. Had Barry been in here? Had he been working on something? Or had Pete done this?

There was a book open facedown in the middle of the junk. Curious, I picked it up. It was a repair manual for the 1996 Wildcat 700 EFI, open to the page showing the wiring diagram and the electrical system.

I knew Pete owned a few snowmobiles but the Wildcat 700 was the fastest. It was an old sled that had seen a rough life and had probably been rebuilt several times. I knew the clutch and the battery could be problems. Was that sled the one they had taken that day? Had the battery finally failed, stranding them in the backwoods? Or had Pete screwed up the repairs?

Back in February when they disappeared, everyone in town had gone out on their sleds or snowshoes to join the search. They had checked every backcountry trail in the county. They had waded through the thick forest on either side. The cops had interviewed everybody and pieced together their last day. Pete and Connie hit the bar for Valentine's dinner and stayed on to party. Around midnight the party turned ugly. At two thirty in the morning, the bartender finally threw them out.

It was snowing hard outside, making it impossible to see more than a few feet ahead in the dark. The snowmobile headlight would have been worse than useless.

Everyone figured they'd headed home and lost their bearings, but no one knew what trail they might have taken. It was two days before Barry reported them missing. By then the snow had wiped out all their tracks.

The rumors about Barry started right away. He'd had lots of run-ins with his father since he'd gotten out of prison. Once he showed up in town with two black eyes. Said he'd walked into a door. It would solve a lot of problems for him if Pete and Connie were out of the way. Even the cops thought so.

I knew they'd been out to search the farm several times before yesterday. They'd tromped through the fields, the barns and the back woodlot looking for bodies. Always without any luck. But I wondered if they'd noticed the repair manual in the shed. And if they had, did they know what it meant? That something might have gone wrong with the sled Pete was driving?

Once again I thought of Constable Swan. She'd listen. She might not even think I was crazy. With my mind on a roll, I crossed the muddy yard and followed the path down to the lake. In shady spots, I could still see snowmobile ruts in the melting snow. It looked as if Pete drove this path often. I stood on the shore and looked across the lake. The pack ice was still solid in the middle of the lake, but it was melted around the edges. Open water was beginning to shine through in sunny spots. Soon it would be gone altogether.

The village of Lake Madrid was just a jumble of specks on the far shore. I could see the white marina, the blue tarps of boats stored over the winter and the steeple of the Catholic church poking through the trees. At the near end of the village, I could see the open water where Silver Creek fed into the lake.

When I was a kid, there was a sawmill on the creek, back in the days before global warming and farm fertilizers turned it into a weedy swamp. Half the village had worked at the sawmill, including Pete. Now the sawmill was a bar, the Lion's Head. It was still home to most of the guys who'd worked in the mill. Even more than the Legion, it was where people got together. They'd come by boat from all along the lake and in winter by snowmobile.

Everybody knew the ice near the creek was tricky. The water ran fast enough that it never really got thick, even in February. People would still go across it. They liked the challenge. Skimming on thin ice, even open water, was a village sport. But you had to know what you were doing, and you needed to see ahead of you. To judge just when to gun the throttle and pull the sled up. It took some skill. And a clear head. Every year a few idiots stoked up at the

Lion's Head before trying their hand at the open water. Live and learn.

Standing on Pete's beach, I could see that the fastest way to get from his farm to the Lion's Head was straight across the lake by the creek. Pete likely did it all the time. But that night, in the pitch black with two people on the sled and a brain full of booze, that was asking for trouble.

Especially if the electronics cut out and killed the engine.

As I stood there, I noticed some tiny dots out on the open water near the creek. Boats? Not moving, just bobbing in place. I squinted. Other, smaller dots floated on the water. I caught my breath. Divers?

Back when the Mitchells disappeared, the police had sent divers under the ice to search the lake bottom off the Lion's Head. In the dark and cold, they found nothing. There was even talk of bringing in sonar from the city, but that never happened.

Not enough evidence to justify the cost, they said. Instead they turned their sights on Barry.

But now that the ice was melting, were the police taking up the search again?

CHAPTER SEVEN

I walked back up to the house. Barry's old pickup was parked crooked in the drive, inches from my dirt bike. I hadn't heard him come back and my heart skipped a beat. The shed door was ajar, just like I'd found it. But had I moved anything in the house? Could Barry tell I'd searched it?

The front door was wide open. I poked my head in. Silence. I tiptoed into the hall and listened. I heard thumps and curses coming from the basement. I was about to sneak away when he came roaring up the stairs, red-faced and swaying. Booze breath hit me from ten feet away.

"You been in the basement, Tool!"

I shook my head. "I finished the kitchen."

"You opened that door, didn't you?"

I don't like lying. My mother used to lie as easily as breathing and I hated it. My face goes all red and my tongue ties in knots. But admitting the truth to Barry right now didn't seem like a good idea either. So I tried to stickhandle through the middle.

"I went down to look at the electrical panel. That knob and tube needs to be replaced."

"I told you not to open that door! Now bad things are going to happen."

"What bad things?"

"There's evil behind that door! You shouldn't have let it out, Rick!"

He teetered on the top stair. I didn't want to grab the guy, because I figured in his mood he'd knock my head off. But I needed to get him away from the stairs. I walked toward the kitchen. "Barry, it's just a door. It's been shut for thirty years."

He didn't follow me. Instead, he balled his fists.

"How do you know how long it's been shut?"

"I don't. I-I just guessed." I eyed the distance between him and the front door. Luckily it was still open. If I moved fast enough, I could get past him before one of those fists connected. "Listen, I gotta go. We need some primer for the walls."

I started into the hall. Barry whirled to slam the basement door shut. "Evil!" he roared.

I seized my chance and ducked outside. "I'll be back tomorrow," I shouted as I grabbed my bike. "I'll pick up the primer on my way."

I don't know if Barry followed me because I didn't look back. Pushing my bike took all my strength and I was down at the highway before it finally caught. I jumped aboard, sweating and gasping for breath. Goddamn, I really needed that truck. The primer and all the other supplies I needed were in the next town. An easy run for the pickup. Not for a dirt bike towing a bicycle trailer.

On my way, I passed by Bud's Garage and saw my truck still sitting in the back lot. It had been there all winter, covered in snow and slowly getting rustier. The sight drove me crazy. The roof was flattened and the tailgate was crushed. Not my fault, but tell that to the bank.

I saw Nancy working in one of the service bays and pulled over. She stopped and came over. Nancy was about ninety pounds of wrinkles and spit. She'd been working in Bud's Garage and Towing since I was born. Been running it on her own since her husband got sick. She could hardly see over the steering wheel of her truck. But she could hitch up an eighteen-wheeler with one hand.

"I heard you're working for Barry Mitchell," she said.

Nothing's a secret in Lake Madrid. I nodded.

"You want to watch yourself. He spends most of his days up at the Lion's Head. If he's anything like his dad..."

I shrugged. "He says he's trying to start over."

"That was Pete's line too. Always starting over, always screwing up."

"I only remember the screwing up part."

"Well..." Nancy gave me a thoughtful look. "He had his good side. Bought Connie the most extravagant gifts every Valentine's Day. She got enough jewelry to start a store."

I remembered the empty box on Connie's dresser. A small thing, but it got me wondering. Where had the jewelry gone?

"Did she ever sell it?"

"If she knew what was good for her, she wouldn't. Pete would want her to parade it around. Not that she went out much. Little mouse of a thing." Nancy sighed. "I guess it's Barry's now, not that he's got much use for it either."

I wondered if he'd already stashed it somewhere out of the sight of lawyers and cops. It would cover his beer expenses till the house was sold.

"Well, it could come in handy. I could use some of that money."

She grinned at my dirt bike. "Don't see why, Rick. With gas prices what they are, you may be on to something here."

"You can't haul lumber with a bicycle trailer. Any chance you can start work on my truck? You know I'll be good for it."

She walked over and together we stood looking at my truck. The winter hadn't improved it. "Money's tight now that Bud can't work anymore, Ricky. I'll need five hundred to buy a roof for you, just for starters."

Last fall my truck had ended up upside down in the creek, with me in it. I'd been too rattled to pay much attention as Nancy hauled it out. Now I had a fresh look. I had some old truck parts in my yard that might do the trick. "Maybe I should just take it home and fix it up myself," I said.

She snorted. "Maybe you should buy a new truck. With the money you make from Barry, I can probably find you something."

If I ever see a penny of it, I thought. But I didn't tell her that. Instead I changed the subject. "Did Pete take his old Wildcat out that night?"

"That's what Barry says, if you believe him. The Cat certainly used to be Pete's favorite. It could really fly."

"Was it in bad shape? Maybe battery or electrical problems?"

She wiped her hands on an old rag and shook her head. "Never saw it. Pete did all his own work on his machines. But he really knew his way around engines and snowmobiles, so I'm guessing he kept it tip-top. He used to come in here some-times for parts or to borrow my tools. Him and Barry." She chuckled. "About the only time I ever saw the two of them get along was when Barry was helping him fix things. Barry used to imitate everything he did, right down to the swagger. Still does from the looks of it."

She headed back toward her garage, where she had an old Jeep up on the lift. "Pete always had a wild streak, and I'm betting drink finally got the better of him. Did some damn fool thing in the middle of a blizzard and sank his sled. Every few years some hotdogger tries that shortcut near the creek and fails. Folks down that end of the village have been hauling them out since the sawmill days."

"Yeah, I saw some boats on the lake today."

"Cops." She picked up a wrench. "Now the ice is breaking up, they'll be looking for volunteers again." She pulled a face. "What some people do for entertainment."

CHAPTER EIGHT

I saw the boats in the bay again on my way over to Barry's the next morning. Half the town seemed to be there. I wondered what Barry was doing. If he was home, what kind of mood would he be in? How do you go about doing a home reno with half the town dragging the lake for your parents' bodies?

But when I arrived, Barry wasn't there. Again. Secretly I was glad.

I'm not a fan of snowmobiles. They're noisy and stinky, and they scare the animals. Give me a sled or skis any time. I even taught Chevy to pull a small toboggan to help me haul firewood and stuff. That's one reason people think I'm a few barrels short of a load.

But I do know engines, and that repair manual in the shed bothered me. Was something wrong with the old Cat? Had Pete tried to fix it and screwed up? What if that *was* the snowmobile he took out that night? If the police knew, they weren't talking.

I parked my dirt bike and went hunting for the Cat. There was a gutted Polaris stashed under the eaves of the barn, and some snowmobile parts in a junk pile worse than mine. I checked the barn. There were tractors, quads and two snowmobiles in there, both smaller and newer than the Wildcat.

Behind the barn I found a smaller shed. I peeked in. Bags of fertilizer, potting soil and lime were piled against the wall. Egg containers full of soil were spread out on the worktable. More pots of soil sat on the ground under dusty fluorescent bulbs. In the back was a small greenhouse full of dried-up plants.

The worktable was cluttered with baggies of seed, each labeled. Sungold tomatoes, green peppers, zucchini, cabbage. Beside them lay a pair of gardening gloves, size small. Both Pete and Barry would be size extra, extra large. So whatever Barry thought, his mother had not spent all her days watching soaps. She had worked out here, getting her garden ready for spring.

I noticed a box taped shut and shoved into the corner under the table. Curious, I pulled it out and yanked off the tape. It was crammed with papers, cards and photos. Bingo.

I sat on the ground and started to go through it. The cards were all sympathy cards. Purple flowers, *Sorry for the loss of your son* and stuff. There was even one from my own mother. *My thoughts are with you,* she said, adding little curls on the *y*'s and a heart underneath. I didn't remember my mother being Connie Mitchell's friend, or anyone else's. She liked her imaginary friends even more than I did.

A stack of report cards came next. Mine had never been great, but the teachers sure didn't pull any punches with Barry. *Aggressive, unpredictable, highly disturbed*, they called him. Then a report from a place called the Children's Care Center, which at least tried to sound like they cared. That was their job. I only understood half the words, but they said Barry was scared, angry and didn't trust anyone.

This must be where Barry had been sent. I read the reports again carefully, trying to make sense of them. The doctors said children often blamed themselves when bad things happen, and Barry seemed to blame himself for his brother's death. As I read that, the paper shook a little in my hand.

I'd had that thought myself. I was nineteen when my mother crashed her car, and I still think I should have driven her that day.

There were more reports from the care center, then some letters from Barry's mother saying the center wasn't helping him. She said he was getting harder to handle. Then Barry's father pulled the plug on the treatment. The doctors disagreed, called Barry a *high risk*. Whatever that meant. But Pete said he could handle his son himself.

Right. With the back of his hand.

I stuffed the papers back in the box, feeling guilty. Had Barry ever seen these reports? Did he know how worried the doctors were? It was none of my business. But something pushed me on. Questions that nagged at the back of my brain. About family secrets, and what lay behind that door.

I reached into the bottom and pulled out a big brown envelope. I knew I shouldn't look inside. It was private.

The envelope was full of photos. There were children blowing out birthday candles, opening presents, hamming it up on tricycles. I looked carefully. I was in some of them, at a birthday party I don't even remember. Barry was in lots of them, looking like The Hulk even back then.

Another little boy kept showing up too. Younger, with baby cheeks and white-blond hair. He and Barry were often together. Two little boys on a rocking horse. At the picnic table. The one under a Christmas tree stopped me cold. The two boys were sticking their tongues out at the camera. Barry had his arm around the littler one. But it wasn't the scowl on Barry's face that stopped me. It was the shirt the little boy was wearing. Hanging over his knuckles, the colors bright and fresh like it was just out of the box.

Green and red plaid.

I shoved the photo back into the envelope and pushed the box away. My heart was hammering. I could hardly think. Was it the same cloth? Or was my mind playing tricks on me? I hid the box back under the table and scrambled to my feet. Listened. In the distance a boat droned. Voices drifted across the lake. But here on the farm, silence.

I peered out the door of the shed. The yard was empty. I thought of the room, the little body, the piece of cloth. I had to know for sure. I ran across the yard and took the basement stairs two at a time. Hoping I could outrun the fear inside me. I yanked the door open, and the loose spike clattered to the floor. Inside, I stared at the bundle in the corner. Was I right about the shirt? It was too dark. Even with a flash-light I couldn't be sure.

I dumped the shriveled apples out of one of the bins and put the skull and the cloth inside. I carried it upstairs into the bright spring sunshine of the yard.

The cloth was spotted with mold, but I could still see the green and red threads of the plaid.

I stared at the skull. Brown, pock-marked and so tiny. I thought of that little white-haired boy. My breath caught, and the bin shook in my hands.

Was I right? All the time the family said he was sick with cancer in the city, was he lying dead in the basement of his own home?

CHAPTER NINE

I felt like I was frozen. Different ideas kept tumbling through my mind. Maybe it was time to go to the police. But what could I tell them? *I think the Mitchells lied about their little boy's death?* What proof did I have? A scrap of rotting cloth, an old photo, a skull that might not even be human? What would they do?

They'd question Barry, for starters. It didn't take too much imagination to see where that would lead. They'd drag up his past and throw even more suspicion on him. Barry, who was just out of prison for assault.

Drinking too much and so freaked out by the basement room that he never went in there. Barry sure as hell wouldn't thank me for bringing the cops down on him.

But another thing was just as sure. I couldn't stand there in his yard forever. He would come back. He would find me with the skull and he would be in a rage. *Highly disturbed.* Those doctors didn't know the half of it.

I wrapped the skull and cloth in my jacket carefully and strapped the bin onto the back of my dirt bike. Then I ran back downstairs to shut the door again. I didn't think Barry would go back into the basement, but I wasn't taking any chances.

I hardly breathed until I was back on my dirt bike, heading down the lane. Just as I turned onto the highway, Barry's truck came flying past me and skidded into his laneway. He gave me three short blasts of his horn, but I waved, hoping I looked cheerful, and carried on. I wasn't stopping for anything. I just prayed I'd hammered the door back well enough that Barry wouldn't find out what I'd done.

I revved the poor bike as high as it could go, putting distance between me and the Mitchell place. The bin was digging into my back. Reminding me I had a problem that needed an answer. Put like that, I knew what to do. Who did I go to whenever I had a problem needing an answer?

The wind picked up as I drove. I was freezing by the time I reached Aunt Penny's grocery store. I hugged the bin tightly as I raced inside. For once the store was empty. I found Aunt Penny at the back, unloading some juice bottles. She straightened up slowly, and for the first time she looked like an old lady. But then she smiled.

"Just in time, Ricky. These are heavy."

I put in a few minutes of work before I told her I needed her help. She didn't say anything, but she gave me the eyebrow.

"Look at this," I said, unwrapping the skull from my jacket.

She peered inside. She sucked in her breath. "What's this?"

"That's what I want to know."

Without batting an eye, Aunt Penny carried the bin to the light. "It looks pretty old."

"What do you think it is?"

"A skull, obviously."

"Human?"

She paused. "Yes, human." She poked the skull with her finger. Her hand was rock steady, but her breathing wasn't. "Where did you find this?"

I hesitated. Aunt Penny was not going to let this ride. That wasn't her style. Her eyes narrowed.

"That's why you were asking about the Mitchells' child, isn't it?"

I nodded and explained about the locked root cellar. I didn't mention Barry and his freak-out. "I found it while I was working down there."

"And you just picked it up and brought it here!"

I shrugged. Aunt Penny wasn't expecting an answer to that. She was on a roll. "Ricky, this is evidence! You tampered with evidence."

"I just wanted to ask you about it. There's other bones too."

"You should have gone right to the police."

"Well, I wasn't sure...It was a long time ago."

She pointed at the skull. Her hand shook now. "This is not an ordinary skull. See this line? It's cracked."

For the first time, in the bright light of her storeroom, I could make out a jagged line through the bone. My mouth went dry. "You think…?"

Aunt Penny finished the thought. "That the skull was cracked? That's for the police to decide. How it got there, and why. Talk to Jessica Swan."

"After all these years, maybe it just dried out and cracked."

She picked up the bit of cloth. "And this? Clothes? A little boy locked in a room? Where's your head?" She laid both the skull and cloth carefully back in the bin. "Put them back exactly where you found them. Exactly. It may be a crime scene. Then go to the police."

Even I watch enough *CSI* with my rabbit-ears TV to know what she meant. But I didn't want to go back into that room. Or face Barry again, once he saw what I'd done. "But if the parents are dead anyway…"

"Barry's not!" she shot back. "Who knows what happened to this poor child? And if the police can't examine the crime scene, how will we ever know?"

She put the bin in my arms and shoved me toward the door. At the last minute, she touched my arm. To my surprise, her voice was soft.

"Go tell Jessica. She won't give you grief."

CHAPTER TEN

I drove down the highway slowly. I hate the mess of other people's lives. I like having just me and Chevy to worry about. Some people think that's lonely, but it's always suited me fine. People complicate things.

Now I was mad at myself. Why did I take on Barry Mitchell's job? Why did I open that basement door? Why didn't I just leave the bones where they were and let well enough alone? Why did I ask Aunt Penny for advice? There was no going back now that she knew. I was going to have to face that room again, face Barry, and lie to the cops about touching the bones.

I shivered. The temperature was dropping. Black clouds raced low over the hills ahead. I saw the police station up ahead on the highway. There were no cruisers out front, but someone was always on the desk. Maybe I should just come clean. Dump the bin on the desk and tell them I moved the skull before I realized what it was.

I slowed and steered my bike into the lot. First I'd see who was on the desk. I knew almost all the cops, and some were nicer than others. I get a lot of teasing around town about my goat, my organic garden and my junk collection. Mostly I shrug it off.

Constable Jessica Swan is another story. I can hardly talk to her. I get all red and my tongue ties in. When she laughs, it's even worse. She's got these big blue eyes that crinkle up. Every thought I have just flies out of my brain.

I pushed open the glass doors to the detachment, scared she'd be the one on the desk. Also scared she wouldn't be. Aunt Penny was right. Jessica Swan wouldn't tease me. She would listen to my story. And she probably wouldn't give me trouble about moving the bones.

It wasn't her on the desk. It was Frank Leger. Frank's got a bad hip and a few months to retirement, so he's on the desk most days. When he works at all. Frank wouldn't want a skull dumped in his lap. Too much work.

He looked up from the sports page and grinned when he saw me.

"She's not here," he said before I opened my mouth.

"Sergeant Hurley in?"

"No one's in, Rick. You want to come back later?"

I knew that's what he was hoping, but I figured I was there. A few questions wouldn't hurt. "Maybe you can help me."

Frank looked wary. "With what?"

"If a case is thirty years old, would the police still investigate?"

"What kind of case?"

"Well…a death."

"What kind of death?"

"I don't know. Maybe an accident, maybe not."

Frank sat back, laughing. "What is it this time, Rick? You kill someone with that exploding scarecrow?"

I went red. I was never going to live down that lawn-mower-powered scarecrow. Every summer there was some joker who ordered one to keep the crows off his cornfield. "No. Just wondering. If I found something and it looked like someone had died, what would the police do?"

"Well, first off, you have to fill out a form." He opened a drawer behind the desk.

I hate forms. Spelling and me don't get along. I backed up. "No, it's not that. I just need to know…How do you investigate? I mean, after all that time?"

Frank sighed. He looked like he was getting tired of humoring me. "You'd be surprised. Crime scene techs can tell a lot. They'll check out the scene. If there's still any evidence, they'll piece it together. Look at the Pickton case. DNA years after the fact. So if you've buried anybody, O'Toole, you'd better confess." Frank laughed.

I made myself laugh. I started to back out the door. "Just curious."

"Can I tell Jess you were looking for her?"

"No." The word was out before I thought. "Yeah, okay."

"Sure thing, Romeo." He laughed again. "You can tell her all about your body."

I was already out the door, hiding my red face.

CHAPTER ELEVEN

As soon as I was back on my bike, I got mad at myself again. I should never have mentioned death. I should have just asked about investigating an old crime. That way I could send the cops down into the room and let them discover the whole scene for themselves. I could hope Frank would forget I mentioned it, but he was having way too much fun with it to forget.

As I headed back toward the Mitchell place, I kept a nervous eye on the angry clouds. I wanted to get the dirt bike safely home before the skies opened up. Now it was past two o'clock and over half the day was shot. If I was lucky, Barry would have left again so I could sneak the skull back into the basement. I detoured down toward the Lion's Head to see if his truck was there.

The town seemed deserted. But down near the bar, two police cruisers blocked the road to the beach, their lights flashing. The sides of the road were lined with parked cars. As I got closer, I saw a huge white police truck with the words *Search and Rescue* on its side. Below it, a line of yellow police tape flapped in the wind. Everyone in town seemed to be there, pressed up against the tape.

On the other side of the tape, there was no one on the beach except cops and paramedics. My stomach did a little flip when I saw Constable Swan's blond ponytail peeking from under her cap. She always looked so tiny even in her Kevlar vest and utility belt. She was standing at the icy water's edge with the others.

No one was talking. Everyone was staring out over the lake. The wind had whipped the open water into whitecaps. All the town boats were gone and there was only one police Zodiac out near the mouth of Silver Creek. It bucked in the waves, fighting the wind. As I watched, two orange buoys popped up in the water. People pointed and started to mutter. Then two police divers surfaced and swam over to talk to the cops in the boat. They turned and gestured a thumbs-up toward shore. Everyone gasped. The muttering grew louder. I could only hear a few words.

"Found it?"

"Sled?"

"What about…?"

An engine rumbled down the road behind me. Even before I turned around

I recognized the knocking pistons of Nancy's flatbed tow truck. Constable Swan jumped into the cruiser and moved it aside to let Nancy pass. The rusty old truck rattled down the hill onto the beach. The crowd parted to let it through, then closed up afterward. I spotted Aunt Penny in the thick of things. I left my bike behind the rescue truck, making sure the skull was well hidden in my jacket. Then I went down to join her.

Something big was happening. I could feel the air crackling. Slowly, carefully, Nancy turned the truck and backed it down to the water's edge. She climbed down without a word. Every scrawny inch of her concentrated on her cables. She unwound them about fifteen feet and handed them to one of the cops wearing bright yellow foul-weather gear and hip waders. Probably one of the Search and Rescue team.

The Zodiac, with the divers aboard now, came ashore, and the divers grabbed one cable each. Nancy was talking to them. Pointing to the truck, holding the hooks and waving her hands. Probably explaining how to work the cables. I'd helped her rig up that winch system.

They must have found something in the water.

Something heavy enough to need a winch.

After a bit, the divers climbed back into the Zodiac and it pushed off. The wind tossed it around like a beach ball. It fought its way back out to the orange buoys. Nancy and the cops stood on the shoreline watching. So did everyone else. The muttering had stopped.

That's when I heard the roar. Kind of like a wounded bear.

There was a scuffle near the back of the crowd. I turned to see Barry shoving his way through. Two cops were trying to hold him back. Even from a hundred feet away, I could see his face, red from cold or booze or rage.

"Not sure he's in shape to see this," I said to Aunt Penny.

She followed my eyes. "Looks like he's already seen that." She nodded toward the edge of the beach. For the first time I noticed the large yellow tarp spread out on the ground beside the paramedics' van. It had a lump in the middle, like there was something underneath. I sucked in my breath.

"Is that one of them?"

She nodded again. She worked her lips like she was trying to get the words out. Normally nothing gets to Aunt Penny, so that was a switch. "Pete," she finally said.

I knew that was coming, but I still felt the blow. I knew how Barry felt seeing the body. No matter how you got along with a parent, something is torn away.

"Looks like he tried to cross by the creek after all, never even made it two hundred yards from the Lion's Head," she said. "Damn fool."

There was a shout from the water. The divers came back up and signaled toward shore. Nancy started her truck and put the winch into gear. The cables slowly grew tight. They quivered and groaned as the winch reeled them in. Dragging whatever they were attached to under the water.

At first I could see nothing. Then the waves began to churn and heave as an object came toward shore. Like a giant shark bubbling through the current. I braced myself. I was expecting Connie's body. Beside me, Aunt Penny gripped my arm. A leg broke the surface. Everyone gasped. I stared as another leg emerged. Then the waves lifted the huge, round, black body and slammed it onto shore.

A snowmobile.

A little laugh ran through the crowd.

Once it was out of the water, Nancy stopped the winch and the cops ran over to look at it. I got only a glimpse of it before it was surrounded. But enough to see the green decals of an Arctic Cat. A vintage Cat.

"Any sign of Connie?" someone shouted from the crowd.

Sergeant Hurley emerged from the group and walked over to Barry. He slipped a blanket over his shoulders. I couldn't hear what he said, but the news spread through the crowd soon enough.

"No sign of Connie yet. But they're sending the divers back out. As long as the light and the weather hold, they'll search the area. Her being lighter, her body probably traveled farther in the current."

Another cop van came roaring down the hill, swerved around the Search and Rescue truck and plowed to a stop inches from the crowd. This one had *Forensic Identification Services* on its side. Two cops jumped out.

"I told you guys to hold the recovery till we got here!" one of them shouted,

still fifty feet away. "We need to photo-
graph the scene as it was!"

"We got your photographs," Hurley
snapped. He was trying to keep his voice
low. He waved at the black clouds. "Look
at that! I didn't want to wait till that came
down on us full force."

"If you screwed up the crime scene..."
the forensic guy said. "If we can't recreate
what happened here..."

Hurley grabbed his arm and led him
over to the snowmobile. I leaned in toward
Aunt Penny. "What's he talking about?
What crime scene?"

She looked grim. "Something was odd
about the way they found Pete. There was
a keg of beer in the luggage bin at the
back, so it would have gone down like a
stone. Pete's jacket was caught on the seat.
So even if he was sober enough, he couldn't
have jumped off in time."

Movement caught my eye. I looked up and saw Barry heading full speed up to the Lion's Head. He yanked the blanket from his shoulders and threw it on the ground. People tried to talk to him, but he brushed them off. I could tell he had only one thing on his mind.

To get blind drunk.

I looked across the open lake to the Mitchell house. My mind was racing. Had Pete and Connie's death been deliberate? Had someone added extra weight to the sled on purpose? Was this another murder that Barry was trying to cover up?

CHAPTER TWELVE

I scrambled back up to my bike. Barry might be good for a few hours in the Lion's Head. But given the mood he was in, he might not stay put anywhere very long. I had to get the evidence back into the basement before he discovered what I'd done. Then I had to notify the police.

The sky was nearly black when I got to the farmhouse. There was still no rain yet, but the wind whipped through the yard. It rattled the windows and howled in the eaves. I shivered. Grabbing the wooden bin, I ran inside and turned on the basement light. I took a deep breath. Barry's fear was getting to me. One more time, I told myself. I hurried down the stairs before I could change my mind. Saw the door and stopped dead.

Barry had barricaded it up. The crowbar was jammed against it. Two-by-fours were nailed across it at crazy angles from top to bottom. It would take an hour to pry them loose. While Barry drank himself deeper into blackness at the Lion's Head.

My thoughts raced. I could just forget the whole thing. Bury the wooden bin somewhere in the yard. Bury the secret of Louie's death with it. No one would know, except Barry and me. And Barry sure as hell wouldn't be telling.

But Aunt Penny would know. So would Frank Leger. He was too lazy to make an issue of it, but it might slip out someday. As a happy-hour joke.

Or he might mention it to Constable Swan.

That did it. Constable Swan believed in the truth. She believed in doing the right thing. I might not be high on her list of cool guys, but I wasn't at the bottom anymore either. She smiled now when she saw me. That was worth everything.

Picking up the crowbar, I began to pry the two-by-fours off. Before long I was sweating. Barry had put at least ten nails into each end. No way evil was getting out. I pried and shoved and pulled and cursed. All the time I could hear the wind wailing around the house. Like a haunting.

I popped the last board off and tossed the crowbar aside. Pulled open the door. Cold rushed out. Its fingers curled around me. I jumped back with a gasp. Get a grip, O'Toole! It's not a ghost. I shone the flashlight inside. It was empty.

I grabbed the bin and stepped into the dark. I felt like dumping the whole thing on the ground and running back out.

But I tried to remember how everything had been laid out. The cops would need to know that. I picked up the little bones to put the cloth underneath. They felt clammy in my hands from the cold earth.

Thunder cracked. I jumped. Listened. I heard another sound. A rumble. More thunder? A car? I scooped the skull out of the bin. Heard the front door bang open.

Fuck! He was here! I dropped the skull on the floor and scrambled out the door.

"O'Toole!"

His voice bellowed through the house. I could hear the rage. The booze. I looked around for a place to hide, but it was no use. He'd seen my bike for sure. I grabbed the storage room door to push it shut, but it stuck halfway. Behind me I heard him thump down the stairs, his breath heavy and stale with beer. I turned around, blocking his view and putting on a big smile. It died the instant I saw him.

He filled the middle of the basement. His eyes were fixed on the dark hole behind me. His hand gripped the crowbar.

"It's been a rough day, Barry. How about I come back—"

He blocked my path to the stairs. "You went in there again!"

I had no answer to that. Couldn't find my voice anyway.

His eyes were bloodshot and his face sagged. "I don't want to hurt you, Rick. But I need to know what you're going to do."

"C-close it up again. That's all."

"Bullshit!" He grabbed my arm with his free hand and hauled me back across to the half-open door. "What did you see in there?"

His grip was like a vise, but I could feel him shaking. "Nothing," I said. "It's just an old root cellar."

He peered inside. Squinted. The skull was sitting plain as day in the middle of the room. "Nooo-ooo!"

The cry made me jump. Fear shot through my gut. Barry began to crash around the basement. "Oh fuck, it *is* there!"

I had no idea what to do. What to say. I just wanted to get out of there.

"It wasn't my fault, Rick! I was just a kid!"

"Sure you were," I managed.

"I don't even remember doing it!" He paced, waving the crowbar. "I just remember this crowbar. My father yelling. Louie just laying there. My mother screaming, 'You killed him!' Over and over again. 'You killed him!'"

Terrified, I began backing toward the stairs. Barry was like a cornered bear, trapped by his memories. Nothing I could say would calm him down. But I had to try. "Let's get away from here, Barry."

He whipped his head back and forth. "All over those stupid chocolates! Dad said it wasn't my fault because I was only a kid. Said he'd take care of it. But, oh Jesus,

I didn't know, I wasn't sure…This is where he put the body!"

I was astounded. Inches from the stairs, I paused. "He never told you?"

"He said we could never talk about what happened. Never tell. Oh God, why did you open that door?" Barry jerked his head up. I froze, one foot on the bottom stair.

"What are you doing, O'Toole?" he roared. He grabbed my arm. Dragged me over to the open door. With one powerful shove, he threw me inside.

CHAPTER THIRTEEN

The force sent me crashing against the wall. I scrambled to my feet just as the door slammed shut. I threw myself at it.

"Barry, what are you doing?"

A hammer began to pound. Through the banging, I heard Barry crying. "Damn it, O'Toole! Why did you open the fucking door?"

Bloody hell! I hammered back. "Forget the door. Forget this room."

"I'm not going back to prison. I can't!"

"You won't. Just let me out." I tried to keep the panic out of my voice. I had to calm him down. "Open the door, Barry."

"This is your fault, O'Toole. It could have been okay, if I'd sold the place. If you didn't open that door."

"Barry! Don't make things worse!"

"I'm going to fix it, O'Toole. Just the way you suggested." His voice grew quiet and his footsteps thudded on the stairs.

I shouted. I pounded. But nothing answered me back. I stood in the dark. Forced myself to listen. Nothing but silence. I fought back panic. Think, Rick. Is there a way to get out of here? I had to see what was around. Had I left the flashlight in here?

I dropped to my hands and knees and began to feel around on the floor. My fingers slid over mason jars, cold earth, the edges of the bin. The small, smooth skull. I jerked back. Reached cautiously again and felt the cold round steel of the flashlight.

I gave a sob. Switching it on, I shone it around the room. Around the frame of the door, which was sealed shut. Along the base of the wall where, long ago, an animal had scratched.

No, not an animal. Little Louie, who had been locked in here alive and had tried to claw his way out. How could anybody be that cruel or, more likely, that stupid?

I knew the answer. If they were drunk enough. And freaked enough to think he was already dead.

Then the flashlight lit up something shiny in the corner. I went closer. Little bits of foil, all in a pile. I dusted one off. It looked like a candy wrapper. Pink. Beside it, some bits of cloth. Not plaid this time, but red. I brought the light close. It looked like part of a big red bow. The kind you see on Christmas presents, or Valentine's boxes.

Valentine! I looked at the pink foil. Valentine's chocolates. Every year Aunt

Penny sold big heart-shaped boxes in her store. My mother used to say some day Elvis would buy her one. Once she even bought a box for herself and pretended they were from him. Didn't matter he'd been dead more than a decade. She ate one a day for a month. Didn't let me near them.

Barry'd said something about chocolates. What had happened? Did Louie get at Barry's chocolates, like any little kid would? And Barry got so mad he hit him? But that didn't make sense. You didn't buy chocolates like this for kids. Not in a heart-shaped box that cost half a week's pay.

Maybe Barry bought them for his mother. Spent every cent he had to get them for her. But the instant I thought that, I knew how ridiculous that was. Barry was five years old. Where would he get the money for chocolates? Only Pete had that kind of money. Pete, who always bought his wife fancy gifts.

But if Pete had bought the chocolates...

I sat in the dark, fingering the foil. I felt like an idea was hanging around just out of reach, in some dark corner. Over my head, I could hear Barry thumping around in the kitchen. I felt my heart racing, my thoughts skittering around like scared chickens. Think, O'Toole. *Think!*

Valentine's Day. Something about that day rang a bell. Then it hit me. Pete and Connie had disappeared on Valentine's Day, after celebrating too hard at the Lion's Head. Too drunk to remember the thin ice at the mouth of the creek. Or so it seemed. But Pete had crossed that ice hundreds of times in the past, and if you gunned the snowmobile fast enough, it was no problem. Even with a keg of beer on the back.

Unless something was wrong with the sled.

Like pinballs falling into slots, the pieces tumbled into place. I didn't breathe.

Someone had tampered with the wiring. Someone who knew they were going to the Lion's Head and would be cutting back home across the lake. Why would Barry do that? Barry hated his father. As a little kid, he'd suffered a lot at his hand. But he was a big man now, and Pete was no match. He'd survived thirty-five years with him. Why now?

Maybe he just wanted the money from the farm. But that seemed like an awful lot of planning for a guy like Barry. And a lot of luck too.

How would he be sure they'd take the Wildcat? How could he be sure the sled would fail at exactly the right time, on the thin ice? Only two people could be sure of that. Pete, if he'd decided to end it all.

And Connie.

Pete really knew his way around engines, Nancy had said. And Barry had helped him.

That was it! That was the idea hanging out there in the dark. Pete and Barry wouldn't need a manual to tamper with the electrical. But Connie would.

"You killed him!" Barry remembered her screaming. He also remembered the crowbar. I picked up the skull and held it under the light. Looked at the crack running through its side. It was a tiny skull, easy to crack with a crowbar. But I had used that crowbar. It was solid iron. A strong five-year-old like Barry could pick it up, but could he lift it over his head? Swing it hard enough to crack this skull?

Impossible. An adult had done this. It had to be Pete. Pete, who was angry about the chocolates. Pete, who had yelled at Louie. Pete, who brought the crowbar down on his head.

And Connie who had killed him for it.

Connie, who'd never stood up for anything in her whole life. Had Pete pushed her one too many times? Had she decided to put an end to their pain?

On Valentine's Day. The day her favorite child was killed, thirty years ago. She'd lived with that ever since, escaping into drugs, cheap novels and gossip rags. Keeping the memories of Louie alive in her private shed.

But Barry didn't know that. He didn't know that when his mother screamed "You killed him," she was screaming at Pete, not him.

And now he was upstairs doing God knows what.

CHAPTER FOURTEEN

"**B**arry!" I pounded on the door. "You didn't do it! Barry!"

A huge bang shook the house. I gasped as a roaring filled my ears. What happened? I pounded louder, but it was no use. The roar drowned out everything else.

I pressed my ear to the door and tried to listen. Held my breath. The blood pounded in my ears. I thought I heard footsteps overhead. Smelled something familiar.

I flashed the light up to the ceiling. Wisps of smoke seeped through a crack in the floorboards. I shone the light on the door. Smoke was sneaking under the door too. The stink of burning wood and rubber filled the room. I yanked off my shirt and stuffed it under the door. Smoke curled across the ceiling. I stared up at the crack. Tried to push handfuls of dirt into the gap, but they wouldn't stick. The tiny room started to heat up. I broke into a sweat.

I grabbed a mason jar and banged it on the ceiling. "Barry! You didn't do it! Your father lied to you!"

Nothing. Dirt fell into my eyes, smoke choked my lungs. I coughed. "Barry!" I screamed, hoarse now. "Your father is the evil one! You can still get out of this. Don't make it worse!"

Overhead, nothing but the roar of the fire. I sank down on the floor. Pressed against the cold earth, I gasped for air. He can't hear me, I thought. The door's too thick. The fire's too loud. And he's probably long gone by now anyway. Setting up his alibi in the Lion's Head.

Rick? What a shame. I didn't even know he was working down there today. But he'd talked about changing the knob and tube, so maybe that's what happened.

I cursed at my own stupidity. I was going to die, and I'd told Barry the perfect way to do it. Turn on the gas stove, flick the overhead light switch, and beat it out the door before the place blows up.

I felt dizzy. I could hardly lift my head. Over the roar of the fire, I heard a distant wail. Angels? My imagination? A trick of my air-starved brain? Was that part of the white light you see just before you die?

The wail grew louder and louder. The light in the room grew dimmer, and my muscles grew limp. Was it coming from outside? Was it real? I dragged air into my lungs. Shouted.

"Help! Down here!"

A siren blasted outside. Another wailed, getting closer. Shouts. Doors slamming. It was real. They were coming to get me!

I coughed and screamed. With my last strength I stood, leaned on the wall, swayed and slammed the jar on the ceiling. Again and again, until it broke. Blood ran down my arm. The fire roared, the water pump thundered to life, blocking out all other sound.

I fell to the floor. Rested my head on the earth, now warm and smoky.

They weren't going to find me. No one could hear me. No one knew about this room, and Barry sure wasn't going to tell them. I was going to die in this tomb like little Louie. Trying to scratch my way out. No one will ever find my body. Like Louie, like Barry's mother. Lost in the huge dark bottom of the lake.

Never to be found.

Darkness began to close. Never to be found. Like the jewelry...

CHAPTER FIFTEEN

A firefighter's ax crashed through the door. Once, twice, three times. Splinters of wood flew in my face.

"See anything?" A woman's voice, dim in my ears. It sounded like Constable Swan.

I tried to lift my head. Tried to speak. "I'm here," I said. But I don't know if the words came out.

"No. It's dark." A shaft of light came through the door. It fell on my face. "Fuck!" The ax went back to work. It was the last thing I heard.

Voices all around me. Pulsing lights. The stink of smoke and the hiss of wet coals. The crackle of a radio. People running. My head ached. My throat was on fire and something pressed down on my face. Nearby someone was crying. Who would cry for me?

I lay still, wondering if I was dead. A finger lifted my eyelid and flashed a light in my eyes. I jerked away.

"He's coming to!"

I blinked. Floodlights lit the whole place like day. The brightness hurt my head. I wanted to sleep. Maybe for a hundred years. But someone was squeezing my arm.

"Rick? Rick! Can you hear me?"

I opened my eyes. Saw the blue uniform of a paramedic and the worried face of Jason Renfold. I'd been at school with Jason, but he'd done a whole lot better than me. Right now I was glad of that.

I tried to move my lips. Cracked and stiff.

"Water," Jason said, snapping his fingers. Next someone was holding a bottle to my lips. Most of the water ran down my chin. I coughed and wished I hadn't. It was like raking a sword up my throat.

"Do you know where you are?" Jason asked.

I squinted around me. Above the bright lights, I saw the darkening sky. I saw smoke and steam hissing from the black skeleton of Barry's house. Nearby I saw cops and firefighters and lots of townspeople. Fires bring the whole town out to help.

I nodded. "Mitchells'," was all I could say. More water was poured down my throat.

I lifted my head. Nearby was a cop car with its door open. I saw Barry inside. He had a blanket over his shoulders and he was crying. Loud and noisy. He stopped when he saw me looking at him. He got out of the car and started toward me. Shoulders hunched, head down, like he was dragging the world. Right away a bunch of cops surrounded him and held him back.

Constable Swan leaned over me. I saw she had a black smudge on her face and bandages on her hands. But she was smiling. "How are you feeling, Rick?"

"Peachy," I said. For that moment, I was.

"Are you up to answering some questions about what happened?"

Jason held up his hand. "We need to get him to hospital. Smoke inhalation can be dangerous. And he has some second-degree burns that need treatment."

"Of course," Swan said. "The questions can wait. The main thing is, you're safe, and the fire is almost out."

Barry blundered forward, a bunch of cops hanging off him. "I told them where you were. I heard you hollering. You always said the wiring on the house was a fire waiting to happen. Right, Rick?"

I looked at him. I could see the fear in his eyes. The hope. I couldn't nod. Couldn't shake my head. I just wanted to sleep. So I shut my eyes.

CHAPTER SIXTEEN

I woke up the next afternoon. I was in a hospital room, with flowers and teddy bears and even a big box of chocolates on the table beside me. It had a card beside it. From Jessica Swan.

Aunt Penny was by the window, talking quietly. I twisted my head to see who she was with. Constable Swan, picture perfect in jeans and blue pullover. With her blond hair loose, she looked like the morning sky. I felt like one big bandage from head to toe. I had an iv line in my hand and an oxygen tube stuck up my nose. I stank like a burning house.

They stopped when they saw me move. Aunt Penny leaned over, her lips tight. "That was a close one, Rick. We spotted the fire from the beach in town, but we all thought the place was empty. If it hadn't been for Barry calling nine-one-one…"

I tried to clear my head. To decide what to say. But it seemed like too much effort, at least for today.

Aunt Penny's lips tightened even more. You'd think it wouldn't hurt the woman to show she was happy.

"What were you doing down there anyway?"

"Um, the bones. I was…"

Aunt Penny sucked in her breath. "The skull. Little Louie."

I nodded. Constable Swan was all business. "What bones? What skull?"

I moistened my lips. It would be a long story, especially for Constable Swan, who hadn't grown up in Lake Madrid and didn't know the family.

Aunt Penny put a hand on my arm. "Don't," she said. "I'll tell her."

So she told Jessica Swan about Louie's death and the cancer story the family made up.

"It seems the little boy's body was in the root cellar all those years," Aunt Penny finished.

"How did he die?" Swan asked. She had taken a notebook out of her purse and was writing things down.

Aunt Penny answered again. "Who knows? It looked to me like the skull was cracked."

Swan frowned. "You saw it?"

"I showed it to her," I forced the words through my raw throat. I wasn't letting Aunt Penny take the heat for this. "I was going to show you yesterday, but then the divers found Pete's body and..."

"And now we may never know," Swan snapped. She pulled out her cell phone and went out into the hall. I could hear her passing the story on to her boss and telling him what the fire investigators should look for.

When she came back in, she still looked mad.

"The fire destroyed pretty much everything, but once the place is cool enough, we'll search it. What does Barry Mitchell know?"

"He was five years old. I don't think he knows much." I felt nervous. Barry was a loose cannon. God knows what he'd tell her under pressure. "But I had a good look around. I think Pete Mitchell hit his son in a fit of rage because he stole some Valentine's chocolates. I don't..." I tried to remember my theory from last night. "I think he was still alive when they locked him down there. But they thought Pete had killed him, so they made up the story about the cancer."

Swan's blue eyes were boring through me. "So he died...down in that hole. Because of some Valentine's chocolates."

I tried to shrug. It hurt every muscle. "That's what I figure. I saw some Valentine's chocolates down there. Pete and Connie disappeared on Valentine's Day, exactly thirty years later. It got me thinking..."

The blue eyes narrowed even more. "Thinking what?"

I was on really thin ice here, unless I dragged Barry into it. "That maybe... maybe..."

"Maybe the deaths are connected?" Swan asked. She was frowning and I could see her mind working. "I had a quick chat with the Ident guys this morning, and it looks as if someone tampered with the kill switch. The switch was still on, but there was a wire connected to it under the hood and running along under the bench. Looked as if someone rigged it to short-circuit the kill switch by pulling the wire."

I remembered the stuff on Pete's work-bench. The tools, the bits of wire, the greasy work gloves and the snowmobile manual, open to the wiring diagram.

I was too tired to explain. But Aunt Penny was on the ball.

"So one yank," she said, "and the snow-mobile would have died. In the middle of the lake."

Swan nodded. "If you timed it right. The Wildcat is a very heavy sled. No question, with that keg on the back, it would go down if the ice was thin."

"Then it had to be someone on the sled," Aunt Penny said. "Pete's been going downhill for years, since losing his job and his child. Maybe he couldn't live with it all anymore and decided to end things for both of them."

"That's what I thought," Swan said. "Until Rick told me about their little boy. Maybe they both decided they couldn't live with their consciences any more. And made a Valentine's Day suicide pact."

I could have left it at that. It tied things up neatly. But the Mitchells came off almost as heroes. There were no heroes in this story. So I called up all my strength. "Why would Pete rig up a wire? If he wanted to stop the sled, he'd just hit the kill switch itself. It's right beside his hand."

Swan pursed her lips in thought. Just then her cell phone rang, and she went back in the corner to answer. But Aunt Penny was still on a roll. "Okay, maybe it was Connie who couldn't live with him anymore, or the memories of what they'd done. This explains why Valentine's Day was such a big deal to them, and why she'd pick that day."

Sure it did, I thought. And the freezing water would make a pretty painless death.

A perfect end. As long as you really wanted to die.

But before I could say anything about the missing jewels, Barry himself filled the doorway. His face was red from the fire and his eyebrows were gone. His eyes looked huge. "Have you found my mother yet?"

Swan was on her cell phone. She looked up, startled. No one had heard Barry come in. She hung up and I could see her sizing him up.

"Not yet, Barry," she said. "It's tricky with the weather and the lake currents."

"But you'll keep looking for her, right?"

Swan gave me a look. It said a lot. I knew she'd figured it out too. How easy it would be for Connie—sitting behind Pete on the sled—to hook his jacket on the seat, jump off the sled and pull the wire as she jumped. Especially if she'd been pushing booze down his throat all evening. I bet she even got Pete to put the keg on the back of the sled too, with a promise of more partying at home. Connie had thought the whole thing out.

"Of course we'll look, Barry. Believe me, we'll look," Swan said. She looked grim. "A person matching your mother's description bought a used snowmobile online on February 12. To be delivered out back of the Lion's Head the evening of February 14. Cash on delivery."

The last piece fell into place. The used snowmobile would've been waiting for her once she'd waded back through the snow. Her final, biggest, escape.

Barry looked confused. I didn't think he'd figure it out on his own. Not now, maybe not ever. I felt sorry for him, but I wasn't going to help him understand. Not for his mother's sake. Not because she'd suffered all her life and finally escaped. Not for his father's sake. That bastard had killed one son and let the other carry the blame for thirty years.

Not for their sakes, but for Barry's.

What was I supposed to say? *No one will find your mother. Unless they look in Florida, LA or New York City. Somewhere as far from this hardscrabble life as her jewels can take her. Somewhere she can disappear without leaving a trace. And without sending you a single sign that she's okay.*

Leaving you to carry the bag. Again.

Next to that, my mother was a peach.

ACKNOWLEDGMENTS

A writer does not work alone. Many people played a role in bringing this book to print. First I am indebted to Bob Tyrrell and Andrew Wooldridge of Orca Book Publishers, not only for their belief in my work but, more importantly, for their vision and commitment to publishing books for reluctant and emerging readers. I'd like to thank my fellow writers Mary Jane Maffini, Sue Pike, Linda Wiken and Joan Boswell, as well as my son Jeremy Fradkin, for their thoughtful critiques of early drafts, and my editor Alex Van Tol for making the final draft the best it could be. Thanks also to Shawn Beckstead of Allan Johnston Repair and Sales in Metcalfe, Ontario, for sharing his expertise on snowmobiles.

Most of all, I owe a huge debt to my parents, Katharine and the late Cecil Currie, for filling my childhood home with books. Without them, I might never have discovered a love of books and a passion to write.

BARBARA FRADKIN is a child psychologist with a fascination for how we turn bad. She is best known for her gritty detective novels featuring Ottawa Police Inspector Michael Green, which have won two Arthur Ellis Best Novel Awards. *The Fall Guy* (2011) was her first book in the Rapid Reads series featuring handyman Cedric O'Toole.